A 3861   DK- BLUE 782

GW00546615

Note to teachers and parents

Through teaching young children, I have found that the association of stories and music increases both the child's enjoyment of the stories and his or her awareness of music. In *Heroes and Heroines* you will find stories each of which is connected with a piece of orchestral music, opera or musical comedy. After each story there follows a section 'About the music' which provides a few simple facts either about the music, the composer or an associated musical topic.

Some ideas for movement to the music are included, though these are purely personal. The child should, I think, be left free to interpret and make different decisions as he or she listens to the music. Similarly, though the music related to a particular story may be only a short extract from a longer work, the actual amount which can be enjoyed will vary from child to child and class to class. Some children can react with enjoyment to almost the whole of the triumphal scene from *Aida*. Others become very bored, very quickly. There are also poems, songs and other stories connected with the main story.

The 'Things to do and make' sections give ideas for art, craft and cookery, which reinforce ideas arising out of the reading or telling of the story. Of course, they only represent a selection of what can be done. The actual possibilities are almost limitless. Diagrams have been added and these together with the accompanying text provide step-by-step instructions which can be followed easily by children without the guidance of an adult.

A cassette is available for use with the stories as much of the music is rather long. The cassette suggests those parts of the music which could be listened to first, although once interest has been aroused many children ask to hear much more.

Finally, it is hoped that listening to the music, reading the stories and working on the activities together will provide an enjoyable pastime, mutually beneficial to both parents and children: through a shared experience adults will find it easier to communicate their own love of music to their children, while for the child, listening to music will become more meaningful and rewarding.

By the same author

Heroes and Heroines in Music

A cassette containing extracts from the music of both books (*Heroes and Heroines* and *More Heroes and Heroines*) is available.

© Wendy-Ann Ensor 1982

First published 1982

ISBN 0 19 321106 8 (paper)
ISBN 0 19 314926 5 (cased)

Printed in Hong Kong

Acknowledgements

We are grateful to the following for permission to reproduce their copyright material:

A. & C. Black Ltd. (14 lines from 'The Policeman' by Clive Sansom from *Speech Rhymes* edited by him); Wm. Collins Sons & Co. Ltd. ('The super-supper march' from *The Cat in the Hat Songbook* by Dr. Seuss with music by Eugene Poddany. Copyright © 1967 by Dr. Seuss and Eugene Poddany. American and Canadian rights: Random House, Inc.); George G. Harrap & Co. Ltd. ('The Muffin Man' from *Music for the Nursery School* arranged by Linda Chesterman); William Heinemann Ltd. ('Spells' from *The Wandering Moon* by James Reeves); Methuen Children's Books Ltd. ('The Alchemist' from *When we were Very Young* by A. A. Milne. American rights: E. P. Dutton. Copyright © 1924 by E. P. Dutton & Co., Inc. Renewal 1952 by A. A. Milne. Canadian rights: McClelland and Stewart Ltd.); Thomas Nelson & Sons Ltd. ('The pirates' tea party' from *Rosemary Isle* by Dorothy Una Ratcliffe); Transworld Publishers Ltd. ('One-eyed Jack' from *One-eyed Jack and Other Rhymes* by Barbara Ireson. A Story Chair book published by Transworld Publishers Limited, London.)

Designed by Ann Samuel
Illustrated by Rowan Barnes-Murphy and Mark Peppé

More HEROES and HEROINES in music

PLAYING TONIGHT

Wendy-Ann Ensor

Oxford University Press
Music Department, Ely House, 37 Dover Street, London W1X 4AH

Oliver

A hundred years ago children who were orphans (that is, they had no mother or father), lived in the workhouse. They were looked after by the man in charge, who was called the Beadle, the Master and several old ladies.

Oliver Twist was born in the workhouse and, as his mother died on the day he was born, he grew up there.

When he was nine years old, Oliver was a pale, thin, little boy. This was not surprising as all the children in the workhouse were half-starved. They only had three small bowls of gruel each day. The gruel was made of oatmeal in water, and they just had water to drink. On Sundays they had half a roll with their gruel. The boys ate in a large stone hall and the Master would stand at one end and give each boy a ladle of gruel into their bowl. They would go back to the wooden table, say grace (a thank-you to God for the food to be eaten), then sit down and eat greedily.

One day the boys were so hungry that one of the older boys said, 'If I don't get some more to eat, I might have to eat one of the other boys.' The smaller boys believed him and were frightened. They decided that they must do something to get more food. The big boy held a handful of sticks and each child pulled one out. Oliver Twist pulled the shortest one and he was told that he must walk up to the Master after dinner that evening and ask for some more food.

Mark Peppé '82

That evening the boys lined up as usual with their small bowls for their helping of gruel. The Master ladled some gruel into each bowl and the boys marched back to their places. Grace was said and they all sat down on the long wooden benches.

After a short time the bowls were empty and all the boys looked towards Oliver. He was very frightened but he was also very hungry. He got up from the table, took his bowl and his spoon, and walked slowly up the long, cold, room to where the Master stood.

'Please sir, I want some more.'

The Master turned pale and held onto the table for support. Nobody had ever asked for more before. He did not know what to say.

'What did you say?' he whispered.

'Please sir, I want some more,' said Oliver.

The old ladies who had been helping the Master stood still in horror and all the children were like statues. Suddenly the Master jumped at Oliver and hit him on the head with the ladle. Then he chased him round the room and screamed for Mr Bumble, the Beadle. Mr Bumble rushed in, listened to the story the Master told him, picked up Oliver and ran out of the room with him.

Now, in the next room were some gentlemen having a meeting and discussing how good the workhouse was to the children, and how it gave them good food and clothes. When Mr Bumble burst into the room with Oliver Twist and told them 'He asked for more' they could not believe their ears.

Oliver was sent to bed in a small room by himself and the next morning a large notice was pinned on the gate of the workhouse. This said that £5 would be

given to anyone who would take Oliver into their home to work for them.

For a week Oliver remained a prisoner in the small, dark, room. There was no bed and he slept huddled in a corner on the cold floor. The next day he was taken to an undertaker where his new master was given £5 and the boy.

However, Oliver was so hungry and unhappy that soon he ran away. He was determined to walk to London, but 65 miles is a long way for a boy of ten to walk, especially when he has hardly any food in him. At night Oliver slept under hedges and haystacks and woke stiff and cold. He was hungry, tired and his feet were sore. Eventually he did reach London where he had some dreadful adventures with Fagin, a very bad man, and his band of thieves.

However, all ended well. Oliver was found by an old gentleman called Mr Brownlow who took him into his home and treated him like a son.

About the music

The story of 'Oliver' is based upon the book *Oliver Twist* by Charles Dickens. Charles Dickens wrote the story more than a hundred years ago and in it he described the unhappiness and misery of children in the workhouse.

Lionel Bart decided to use the story to make a musical. This was a great success and it was still showing at a London theatre after ten years. Many of you will also have seen the film on television.

Listen to two of the most popular songs from the show. One is 'Food, Glorious Food' which the boys in the workhouse sing when they are so hungry. The second tune is 'Who will buy this Wonderful Morning' which is sung when all the street criers and traders are trying to sell their pears, cherries, knives and other goods in the streets of London.

Oliver in the workhouse

Here is a song about being hungry. Do you remember how Oliver was so hungry when he was in the workhouse that he said 'Please sir, I want some more.'? In this song there are many different kinds of foods to sing about – some you will have heard of and others which are quite extraordinary!

When you have heard the song, you will know that it is a steady march. Pretend you are a band. Choose drums, cymbals, triangles or bells and march round in time to the music. See if you can learn the exciting and funny words and sing them at the same time.

The super-supper march

The workhouse was full of children who were unhappy and very hungry. The nursery rhyme about an old woman who lived in a shoe tells how she also had so many children that she didn't know what to do with them. Do you remember this nursery rhyme?

There was an old woman,
Who lived in a shoe.
She had so many children,
She didn't know what to do.
She gave them some broth,
Without any bread,
Then whipped them all soundly,
And sent them to bed.

Oliver in London

When Oliver lived in London, many people brought their goods round to houses to sell them. Men and women selling hot cross buns would call or sing in the streets to tempt someone to buy them.

Here is a song about hot cross buns which you probably know.

Hot cross buns

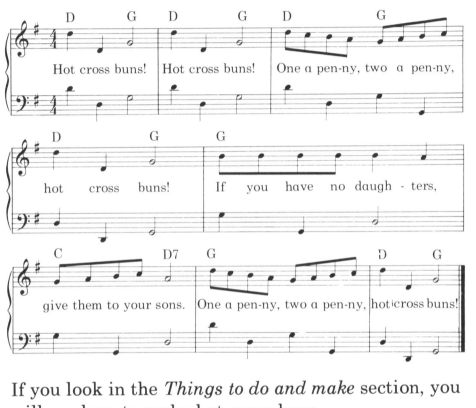

If you look in the *Things to do and make* section, you will see how to make hot cross buns.

Here is a song that Oliver might have heard in London. The Muffin Man used to carry a large tray of muffins on his head and ring a bell to call customers to him. Muffins are a kind of tea-cake which is eaten hot with butter. Drury Lane is a famous street in London.

The Muffin Man

1. Do you know the Muf-fin Man, The Muf-fin Man, The Muf-fin Man,

Do you know the Muf-fin Man, Wh[o] lives in Dru-ry Lane?

2. Yes! We know the Muf-fin Man, The Muf-fin Man, The Muf-fin Man

Yes! We know the Muf-fin Man, Who lives in Dru-ry Lane.

Cries of Old London

Oliver would have seen men and women selling many different things in the streets and calling out these songs to make people come and buy them.

Here are some of the traditional cries of Old London. Read them carefully and then imagine you are one of the sellers singing out your special song.

Lavender lady

Sweet lavender! Sweet lavender!
Who'll buy sweet lavender!

Broom seller

New brooms, maids, new brooms!
Buy my brooms,
To sweep your rooms,
New brooms, maids, new brooms!

Now choose which you would like to sell and learn the words. When you know your words, you can make some of the goodies out of dough. Look in the *Things to do and make* section for the recipe to make modelling dough.

Pear seller

Pears for pies,
Come feast your eyes!
Come feast your eyes!
Ripest pears,
Of every size.
Who'll buy?
Who'll buy?

Tinker

Have you any work for a tinker, mistress?
Old brass, old pots, or kettles?
I'll mend them all with a tink, terry tink,
And never hurt your metals.

Apple seller

Here are fine golden pippins,
Who'll buy them, who'll buy?
No one in London sells better than I,
Who'll buy them, who'll buy?

Things to do and make

Lavender bags

One of the street cries of Old London was sung by the Lavender Lady. She said:

'Sweet lavender! Sweet lavender!
Who'll buy sweet lavender?'

Many people grow lavender in their gardens. You could make lavender bags.

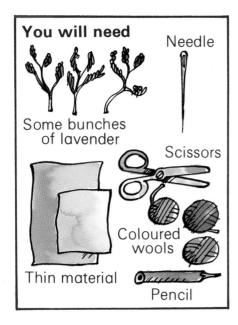

You will need

Some bunches of lavender

Needle

Scissors

Coloured wools

Thin material

Pencil

1 Gather bunches of lavender. Tie round with string and hang to dry.

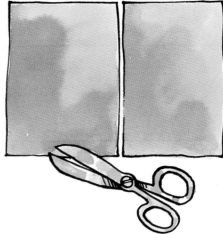

2 Cut two shapes from the thin material 13 cm × 18 cm.

3 Draw a picture on the material with the pencil.

4 Embroider your picture with different coloured wools.

5 Stitch the three sides of your material together to make a bag.

6 Run a thread through the top of the bag to close it, leaving two long ends of thread.

7 Put the lavender heads into the bag and draw up with the thread to close it.

8 Lavender bags make ideal presents, and, if you put one with your clothes in a drawer, it makes everything smell lovely.

A bowl for nuts and sweets

When Oliver asked for more, he held up his little bowl. You can make a bowl and use it for your crisps or nuts or sweets.

You will need

plasticine or clay

a pencil or stick

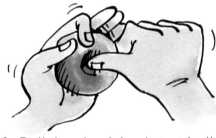

1 Roll the plasticine into a ball, put it in the palm of your hand, and make a hole with the thumb of your other hand.

2 Turn the ball round and round and gradually make the hole larger. Try to keep the outside smooth and round.

3 When you have made a smooth bowl with a large hole, put it somewhere safe and leave it to get hard.

4 Now take your pencil or sharp stick and make some patterns on your bowl.

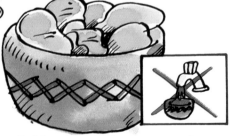

5 Your bowl is now ready to use for your crisps or nuts or sweets. Do not put water or any other liquid in the bowl.

Hot cross buns

When you have sung your song about hot cross buns, you might like to make some. Here is the recipe.

1 level teaspoon sugar

¼ pint warm milk

½ level teaspoon salt

1 egg

2 oz sugar

2 level teaspoons dried yeast

12 oz plain flour

1 oz margarine

½ level teaspoon mixed spice

1 oz dried fruit

1 oz fat and 2 oz plain flour for the pastry crosses

1 Stir the sugar into the milk, sprinkle the yeast on top, stir and leave for 10–15 minutes, until frothy.

2 Sift the flour and salt and rub in the fat. Stir in the 2 oz sugar, mixed spice and the dried fruit.

3 Break the egg into a basin and whisk with a balloon whisk.

4 Make a well in the flour, pour in the milk, yeast and egg; gradually mix in the flour to form a soft dough, then knead well until it is smooth.

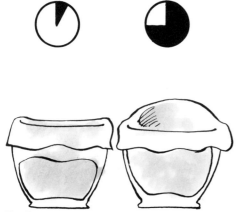

5 Cover with a cloth and leave in a warm place to rise, until the dough has doubled in size.

6 Then turn it onto a floured board and knead lightly. Divide into ten pieces and put on a baking tray.

7 Cover and leave in a warm place until the buns look puffy.

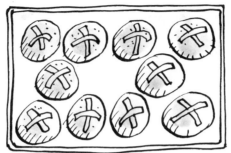

8 Rub 1 oz fat into 2 oz plain flour, add a little cold water. Knead lightly and then roll out thinly, cut into strips about 10 cm long.

9 When the buns have risen, damp the strips of pastry and put two on each bun to make a cross.

10 Bake at the top of a hot oven (425°F, Reg. 7) for 15–20 minutes until golden brown.

Modelling dough

When Oliver was watching the people selling their goods in the streets of London, he would have noticed that they carried trays showing the things they were selling. You could make the different foods from dough and then have something to sell when you sing your songs. Here is the recipe for making modelling dough.

You will need
1½ cups of salt
2 cups of water
3 cups of flour
1 cup of powder paint

1 Mix salt, flour, water and powder paint together.

Now make some food; you could make pears, nuts, apples, cherries and strawberries.

2 Now make some food; you could make pears, nuts, apples, cherries and strawberries.

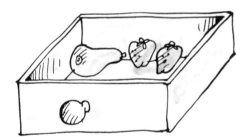

3 If you want to keep the things you have made then put the dough in a safe place where it will dry out and harden.

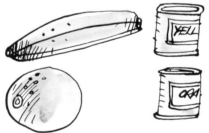

4 If you want to make different coloured food, you can use different coloured powder paint.

5 Now you can use your food to sell when you sing your Cries of Old London.

Finger puppets

Oliver lived in the workhouse with a lot of other children. You could make some finger puppets to play with and pretend they are Oliver and his friends.

You will need

One old glove

Pieces of coloured felt

Different coloured wools

Strong glue

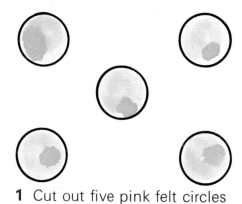

1 Cut out five pink felt circles about 3 cm across.

2 Glue one on to each fingertip of the glove.

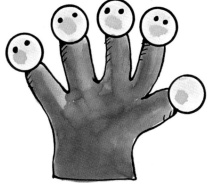

3 Cut out ten small circles in dark felt for the eyes. Glue on to the faces.

4 Cut five red felt pieces for the mouths. Glue these on to the faces.

5 Now choose different coloured wools to glue on for the hair. Some could be long and some short.

6 Cut out clothes from the felt, shirts and trousers for the boys, dresses for the girls. Glue into place.

7 You could cut out buttons, make bow-ties for the boys, bows for the girls' hair and glue them on.

8 Put on the glove and you can make Oliver and his friends dance to the music.

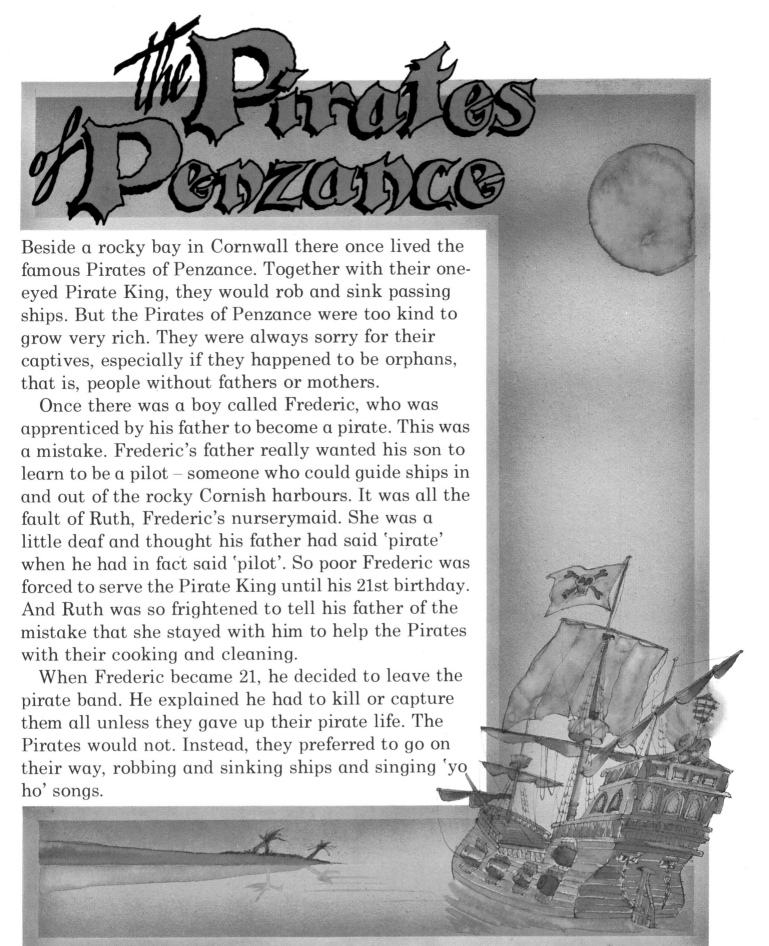

The Pirates of Penzance

Beside a rocky bay in Cornwall there once lived the famous Pirates of Penzance. Together with their one-eyed Pirate King, they would rob and sink passing ships. But the Pirates of Penzance were too kind to grow very rich. They were always sorry for their captives, especially if they happened to be orphans, that is, people without fathers or mothers.

Once there was a boy called Frederic, who was apprenticed by his father to become a pirate. This was a mistake. Frederic's father really wanted his son to learn to be a pilot – someone who could guide ships in and out of the rocky Cornish harbours. It was all the fault of Ruth, Frederic's nurserymaid. She was a little deaf and thought his father had said 'pirate' when he had in fact said 'pilot'. So poor Frederic was forced to serve the Pirate King until his 21st birthday. And Ruth was so frightened to tell his father of the mistake that she stayed with him to help the Pirates with their cooking and cleaning.

When Frederic became 21, he decided to leave the pirate band. He explained he had to kill or capture them all unless they gave up their pirate life. The Pirates would not. Instead, they preferred to go on their way, robbing and sinking ships and singing 'yo ho' songs.

Soon Frederic heard singing. There, coming towards him over the beach, was a family of beautiful girls. Apart from Ruth, they were the only girls he had ever seen, and he was determined to marry one of them. Not wishing to frighten them with his pirate costume, Frederic hid in a cave. But when they started to paddle in the sea, he jumped out and asked if one of them would marry him. They all said 'no' except Mabel. They were so busy talking that they did not notice the Pirates had returned. Suddenly from behind every rock a pirate appeared, a black patch over his left eye and a knife in his mouth. Frederic and the girls were captured and the Pirates announced they would each marry one of Mabel's sisters.

At last Mabel's father, Major-General Stanley, appeared, climbing slowly over the rocks. He was surprised and not very pleased that his daughters were all going to marry pirates. Suddenly he had a brainwave. 'Surely,' he said, 'you are not going to rob me of my daughters and leave me alone. Don't you know that I am an orphan'. This, of course, was untrue, but the Pirates believed him. Immediately all the girls were set free to go home amid the usual singing and dancing.

On a clear moonlit night some time later, Frederic was getting ready with a band of brave policemen to set out and capture the Pirates. They met together near an old ruined chapel near the castle where Mabel lived. Mabel and her sisters sang songs to wish them success and tell them how brave they were. They did not want to go and fight the Pirates of Penzance, although of course in the end they went.

Just then Ruth and the one-eyed Pirate King appeared from behind a rock.'When were you born?' they asked Frederic. 'On the 29th February, 21 years ago,' he replied. Then he realized the terrible truth. Since the 29th February comes only once in every four years, he would not reach his 21st birthday until he was 84 years old. He was therefore still a pirate and so could not kill his pirate friends. With a sad goodbye to Mabel he left to join them.

Meanwhile, the policemen were left to protect Mabel and her father and to try and capture the Pirates. But they were unsuccessful and were forced to kneel in surrender at the foot of the terrible Pirate King. All seemed lost.

However, the story has a happy ending. The Sergeant of Police told the Pirates to give in in Queen Victoria's name. Strange though it may seem, they all gave in. Then Ruth explained that they were not really wicked pirates who killed people and stole things, but noblemen in disguise. General Stanley, Mabel's father, ordered them to be sent to the House of Lords instead of to jail. Thus Frederic and Mabel were able to marry after all and lived happily ever after.

And the Pirates? They took off their pirate costumes, put on dark suits and started to catch the 8.08 train each morning to London. If you go there and look very carefully, you might even see one.

About the opera

The Pirates of Penzance is an operetta. It was first performed about one hundred years ago in 1879. An operetta is a short opera with a spoken 'dialogue' which means that the conversation between the singers is often spoken and not sung. It is rather like what we call a musical, like *My Fair Lady, Oliver* or *Evita*. The story of the Pirates of Penzance was written by William S. Gilbert and the music by Arthur Sullivan. Together they wrote 13 very funny operettas.

Listen to a record or tape of the Pirates of Penzance. Begin with *A Rollicking Band of Pirates We* about three-quarters of the way through Act II. The voices of the Pirates are heard off stage and the policemen hide. The Pirates enter singing. The Major-General enters in his dressing-gown and sings softly. Then his daughters enter and sing together.

The Pirates spring out of their hiding place and seize the General and the girls. Suddenly the police appear. There is a short, sharp fight, the police are overthrown and kneel to surrender with the Pirates standing over them.

The Sergeant of Police asks the Pirates to give in in the name of Queen Victoria.

The Pirates obey and now kneel in surrender with the police standing over them. The General tells the police to take the Pirates prisoner but Ruth tells him that they are not real pirates but noblemen who have gone wrong. The Major-General forgives them and says they may marry his daughters.

● Now divide into four groups:

Group 1 The Pirates and the Pirate King. These pirates are jolly, noisy and full of fun. Carry shakers and tambourines. If you can find some scarves, wrap them round your heads and see if you can find large gold earrings.

Group 2 You are the policemen. You are rather slow and heavy. Shuffle your feet and tap slowly on the drums.

Group 3 The General's daughters; you are Mabel and her sisters. You are running gaily along, chattering as you go. You carry clappers and bang them lightly in time to the music.

Group 4 You are the Major-General. He is rather sad when he thinks his daughters are going to marry pirates. However, when he knows the pirates are really noblemen in disguise he becomes very pleased and excited. You can play the cymbals when you are sad, but when you are pleased you can play the triangle.

Frederic was born on the 29th of February. Once in every four years the month of February has 29 days instead of the usual 28; therefore in these years there are 366 days instead of 365. These years are called Leap Years.

Here is a rhyme about the months.

Thirty days hath September,
April, June and November:
All the rest have thirty-one,
Excepting February alone,
Which has but twenty-eight days clear,
And twenty-nine in each Leap Year.

Peter Pan

Another story which has lots of pirates in it is *Peter Pan* by J.M. Barrie.

This is a story about a little boy who never grew up. His name was Peter Pan and he came from a make-believe island called the Neverland. It is also a story about the Darling family – Mr and Mrs Darling, their three children, Wendy, John and Michael and their nurse, who was a large dog called Nana.

One night when Mr and Mrs Darling were out and Nana was in the garden, a window flew open and a little boy blew in. It was Peter Pan, followed by the fairy, Tinkerbell. He had come to ask Wendy to come with him to the Neverland to rescue the Lost Boys – boys who had fallen out of their prams while no one was looking after them. 'I will teach you all how to fly,' he said. So he sprinkled some fairy dust on John and Michael and soon they were flying around the bed-room in great excitement. Wendy still hesitated, especially when she heard there were pirates in the Neverland. 'Pirates,' said John. 'Let's go at once!' And he seized his Sunday hat and flew out of the window. Just as the three children and Peter flew away over London, Mr and Mrs Darling rushed into the room. They were too late.

On the way, Peter told the children about the pirates and their leader, Captain Hook. He told them how he had cut off Hook's hand in a fight, so that now the Captain had an iron hook instead of a hand!

Suddenly, there was a tremendous crash. The pirates had fired their large gun 'Long Tom'. No one was hurt, but Wendy was blown upwards.

In the middle of the pirate band rode Captain Hook. He had long black curls and deep blue eyes, and instead of a right hand he wore a hook. More than anything he wanted to kill Peter Pan, for, as he explained to Smee, his faithful pirate friend, Peter had cut off his hand and thrown it to a crocodile. The crocodile liked the taste of Captain Hook's hand so much it wanted to eat the rest of him and it followed behind the pirate band hoping for a leg or an arm next time. Luckily, the crocodile had also swallowed a clock with a very loud tick so that as it moved Captain Hook could hear 'tick, tick' and escape.

'Some day,' said Smee, 'the clock will run down and then the crocodile will get you.'

'Yes,' said Hook, 'that's what I'm afraid of.'

After many days and nights Wendy, John and Michael decided they must go home to see their parents. Wendy said she would take all the Lost Boys with her, but Peter would not go. He said he always wanted to be a little boy and to have fun. If he found a mother she might make him grow up too quickly.

Just as they were saying goodbye, there was a terrible noise. The pirates had attacked the Indians, who also lived on the island. The fight was terrible and many Indians died. Wendy and the Lost Boys were dragged on board the pirate ship. Soon, Smee and his mates were preparing the plank that the boys were to walk that night. Wendy was brought on deck to watch.

Suddenly – 'tick, tick, tick!' very close. It was the crocodile and every head turned towards Hook. He crouched in a corner, very white and trembling. The crocodile had come for him. Actually, although the crocodile *was* swimming around in the water, his clock had run down and it was Peter Pan who was making the ticking noise and had climbed on board.

The pirates and the boys fought for a long time. Then, suddenly, Hook lost his sword and jumped overboard into the mouth of the crocodile. The rest of the pirates all swam safely away and Wendy, John, Michael and the Lost Boys flew home happily to live with Mr and Mrs Darling and Nana. Peter went to live with Tinkerbell. He did not want a mother who would make him grow up too quickly. He wanted to be a little boy for ever and have fun.

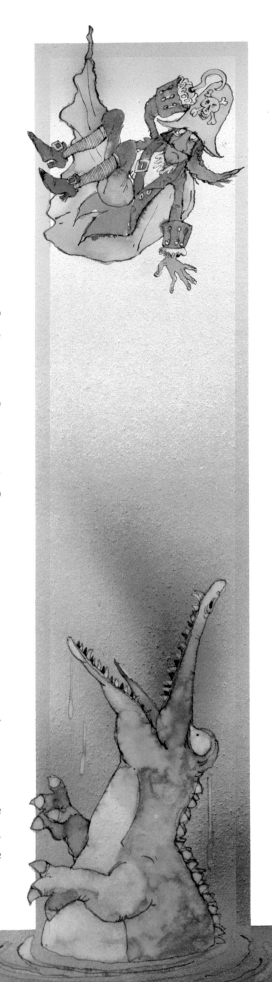

About pirates and policemen

Real pirates were often very nasty people who killed, sank ships and stole, just to grow rich. They were more like the Pirates of Neverland than the Pirates of Penzance.

Here is a poem about some rather nice pirates.

The pirates' tea party

We'd ever so many kinds of cake,
And at least three sorts of jam;
Doughnuts and cucumber sandwiches,
Some made with chicken and ham;
Scones and parkin and honey had we,
The day that the pirates came to tea.

The oldest he had twinkly eyes,
A deep sword-slash on his cheek,
A stubbly beard that was hearty red,
He hadn't washed for a week.
He showed me his cutlass sharp and bright.
He slept with it 'twixt his teeth at night.

The second he was thin and fair,
He blushed when they yelled at him;
Tho' young he had killed a dozen Turks,
They called him Terrible Tim.
He wore a handkerchief round his head,
Purple and yellow with spots of red.

The third was merely a boy from school,
And although he wore a belt,
A pistol in it and high sea boots,
And a frightful hat of felt,
He is just pretending that he is one,
With his 'Yo, ho, ho' and 'Son of a Gun!'

DOROTHY UNA RATCLIFFE

22

'A policeman's lot is not a happy one,' sings the policeman in the Pirates of Penzance.

Here is a poem about a rather stern policeman.

The noise that annoys,
All the naughty little boys,
Is the tramp of the feet,
Of the policeman on his beat,
As he walks up and down,
With a frown, with a frown,
As he walks up and down,
With a frown.

When he holds up his hand,
All the traffic has to stand.
Every car, every bus,
Has to stop without a fuss.
They must wait in a row,
Till the policeman tells them, 'Go!'
They must wait until the policeman
Tells them, 'Go!'

One-eyed Jack

Here is a song about One-eyed Jack, the pirate chief.
He also wore a hook, just like Captain Hook.

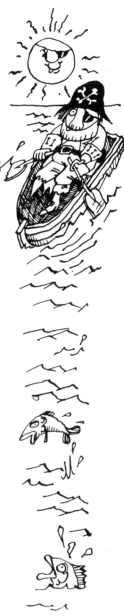

23

Things to do and make

When you have made some puppets you can act the story of the Pirates of Penzance while listening to the music.

The pirate

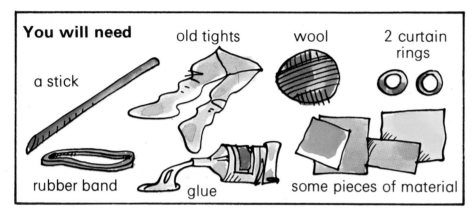

You will need

a stick

old tights

wool

2 curtain rings

rubber band

glue

some pieces of material

1 Cut the toe off the tights. Stuff this with pieces of tights to make a ball.

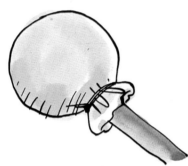

2 Put the end of the stick in the ball and fasten with a rubber band.

3 Cut some lengths of wool for hair and a beard and glue on to the head.

4 Cut out an eye, a black patch for the other eye, a nose and mouth, and glue on to the head.

5 Cut out a semi-circle of material for a cloak and glue around the stick.

6 Cut out a triangle for a scarf and tie around the head. Cut out and glue on some coloured spots.

7 Glue or sew on the curtain rings for earrings.

The policeman

1 Do *not* give your policeman a beard. Make a cloak in blue and glue around the stick.

2 Cut out two hat shapes, glue the sides but not the bottom, then glue on to the head.

3 Cut out a badge in yellow and glue on to the hat.

Mabel

Now you can make a girl like Mabel and her sisters.

1 Make her eyes and mouth larger, and her hair much longer.

2 Cut out two dress shapes, glue them together around the stick.

3 Cut out two hand shapes, glue them on to the bottom of the sleeves.

The Major-General

If you are making puppets to act to the music, you must include the Major-General.

1 Make the Major-General a moustache, instead of a beard, from short pieces of wool.

2 Cut out two red coat shapes, glue together around the stick. Cut out and glue on two hands.

3 Cut out two black hat shapes, and glue on. Make a white frill edging and glue around the edge of the hat.

Some pirate food

In the poem *The pirates' tea party* there were many kinds of food mentioned. Here is the recipe for making scones.

Scones

You will need

8 oz plain flour

¼ pint milk

2 level teaspoons cream of tartar

1 egg   1 oz margarine

1 level teaspoon bicarbonate of soda

a cutter

1 Sieve cream of tartar, bicarbonate of soda and flour into a bowl.

2 Rub the fat into the mixture until it looks like breadcrumbs.

3 Make a well in the middle of the mixture and gradually add the milk.

4 Turn the dough out onto a floured board. Knead well.

5 Roll out to about ½ inch thick.

6 Cut into rounds with the cutter and put them on a greased tin.

7 Break the egg and beat well, brush the rounds with egg, bake in a hot oven (425°F or Reg. 7) for 10 minutes.

The Pirates also ate doughnuts at their tea party.
Here is a recipe for making doughnuts.

Doughnuts

You will need

10 oz plain flour

1 egg

4 tablespoons milk

½ oz melted lard

1 level teaspoon baking powder

2½ oz caster sugar

3 inch cutter

1½ inch cutter

fat for frying

1 Sift the flour and the baking powder.

2 Beat the egg and mix with the sugar, milk and lard.

3 Stir into the flour and mix to a dough.

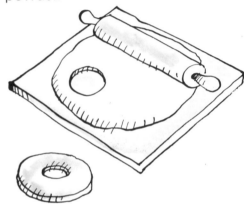

4 Roll out on a floured board and cut into rings using the two cutters.

5 Now ask a grown-up to help you fry the doughnuts. Hot fat is very dangerous.

6 Heat the fat and fry the doughnuts, turning them once, until crisp and golden.

7 Drain on kitchen paper, toss in sugar and serve.

27

The Little Sweep

Not so long ago, the only way to keep warm at home in winter was to light a fire. Homes were built with a fireplace in each room and the first job of the day was to clean the fireplace. The fire was warm and bright and people would sit beside it and work or read or tell stories. But it also made smoke and dirt. Once a year in the spring, all the chimneys were cleaned to get rid of the black soot from the winter fires and the person who did this job was the chimney sweep.

You may have seen a chimney sweep with a van and long brushes and a vacuum machine, but there was once a time when the sweep would also have had a small boy – a little sweep to help him clean the chimneys.

This is the story of a little sweep called Sam.

In about the year 1810 Sam, who was eight years old, was sold by his father to Black Bob. Black Bob was a chimney sweep who needed a small boy to climb up the inside of the narrow chimneys in big houses with a small brush to clean where Black Bob's big brushes would not reach. The work was hard. Sam often finished his work burnt and bleeding and he was always afraid of getting stuck in the chimney.

One day, Black Bob sent Sam up a chimney at a great house in Suffolk called Iken Hall. The chimney was narrow and twisty and Sam climbed with a rope tied round him in case he got stuck. He pushed and struggled up, with his brush cleaning the choking soot from the chimney until, at one particularly narrow corner, he became absolutely stuck.

Now there were three children living at the Hall called Juliet, Gay and Sophie. Their mother and father were away and to keep them company they had three friends, Johnny, Hughie and Tina Crome, staying for a holiday, and Rowan who looked after them. There was also Miss Baggot, the housekeeper of Iken Hall, but the less said about her the better!

The children were all playing hide and seek when they heard Sam's cries. They found the end of his rope leading out of the fireplace and all together they pulled and pulled and down came Sam. The children decided that Sam must not go back to Black Bob. He must hide. So they made a great mess of soot by the window so that Miss Baggot and Black Bob would think Sam had run away. Later the children brought Sam out of a secret cupboard and gave him a magnificent, beautiful bath.

But how could the children help Sammy escape?

They had to think quickly for soon Miss Baggot would be back and if she found Sammy, she would be sure to give him back to Black Bob. Suddenly someone thought of the trunks. Tomorrow the Crome children must all return home and Rowan could pack Sam into one of the trunks which would carry their clothes, books and toys. The trunks were much bigger than suitcases and there would be just room for Sam to hide. Once home they were sure that their mother and

father would help Sammy because they hated the way little children had to clean chimneys. Until the morning Sam could hide in the cupboard.

Sam hid in the secret cupboard all night and in the morning the children brought him an enormous breakfast of ham and eggs. One of the trunks was unstrapped and Sammy climbed inside with a bag of money from Juliet, Gay and Sophie, the children who lived at the Hall, and also some bread and butter in case he was still hungry. Soon Alfred and Tom climbed the stairs to fetch the trunks, out of breath for the stairs were steep, with Alfred complaining about his bad back. But why was this one so heavy? What could be inside it? It must be unpacked they said, or left behind.

'Oh, no,' cried the children.

'Yes, you must unpack it,' said the two men.

'Let us all help you lift it,' said Rowan.

So Rowan and all the children heaved the trunk to the top of the stairs. Then slowly and gently, because Sammy was inside, down the stairs, across the landing, down more stairs and finally out to the waiting coach. Johnny, Hughie, Tina and Rowan climbed aboard. Tom cracked his whip and the old coach trundled slowly out of the Hall gates.

It was the end of a holiday for the three children and Rowan. It was the beginning of a new life for Sammy.

About the music

Benjamin Britten was born in 1913 in Suffolk in England, and died in 1976. He started to write music when he was five years old. He wrote many operas, orchestral pieces and songs. *The Little Sweep* is part of an opera in which seven children and four adults make up a story, write the words of the opera and also the music.

There are four main songs in the opera and two of these have been chosen for you. First listen carefully to them, and then dance and move to the music.

The Sweep's Song

This is the first song in *The Little Sweep* and it introduces the opera. Listen carefully to the sweeping sounds that the music makes as everybody sings.

● Divide into three groups.

Group 1 You are the small boys who climb the chimneys to sweep the difficult parts where the brushes cannot reach. Stretch your arms and legs and climb carefully.

Group 2 You are the masters who send the boys up the chimneys. You also push the tall brushes up to clean the chimneys. Stretch as tall as you can to push your brushes up the chimney.

Group 3 You are the people walking around and watching the chimneys being swept. Two people take the cymbals and listen carefully when to clash them. The rest walk round beating the drums.

Now change groups and move to *The Sweep's Song* again.

The Coaching Song

This is the last song in *The Little Sweep*, when Sam is safely in the coach with Johnny, Hughie and Tina Crome and Rowan. Tom has cracked his whip and the old coach has trundled slowly out of the Hall gates.

● Choose two children. Take four half coconut shells. You will bang the shells together to sound like horses' hooves. Try to keep the rhythm steady with 'clip clop' noises in time to the music.

  Choose one child to be Tom. Fetch the clappers, Tom. Use the clappers to crack the whip to make the horses gallop faster.

  All the rest of the children take the bells. You are the horses. You will gallop round to the music shaking the bells.

About chimney sweeps

The idea of *The Little Sweep* came from a poem called *The Chimney Sweeper* by William Blake. Here it is.

The Chimney Sweeper

When my mother died I was very young,
And my father sold me while yet my tongue
Could scarcely cry, 'Weep! weep! weep!'
So your chimneys I sweep, and in soot I sleep.

There's little Tom Dacre, who cried when his head,
That curl'd like a lamb's back, was shav'd: so I said,
'Hush, Tom! Never mind it, for when your head's bare,
You know that the soot cannot spoil your white hair.'

And so he was quiet, and that very night,
As Tom was a-sleeping, he had such a sight!
That thousands of sweepers, Dick, Joe, Ned and Jack,
Were all of them lock'd up in coffins of black.

And by came an Angel who has a bright key,
And he open'd the coffins and set them all free;
Then down a green plain, leaping, laughing, they run,
And wash in a river, and shine in the sun.

Then naked and white, all their bags left behind,
They rise upon clouds and sport in the wind;
And the Angel told Tom, if he'd be a good boy,
He'd have God for his father, and never want joy.

And so Tom awoke, and we rose in the dark,
And got with our bags and our brushes to work,
Tho' the morning was cold, Tom was happy and warm;
So if all do their duty they need not fear harm.

The Water Babies

Here is a very well known story by Charles Kingsley about another little sweep called Tom.

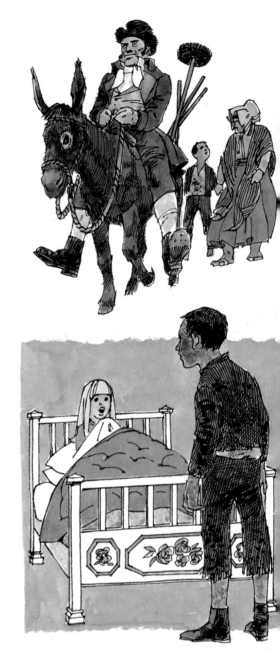

Once there was a chimney sweep whose name was Tom. He lived in a town where there were many chimneys to sweep and much money to be earned for his master, Mr Grimes, to spend. But Mr Grimes was a cruel and mean master and used to beat Tom until he cried.

One morning, Tom was following his master along the road to a very big house when they met an Irishwoman. She was wearing a grey shawl, a red skirt, but no shoes or stockings. Mr Grimes offered her a ride on the donkey but she said, 'No, thank you. I will walk with Tom.' Tom enjoyed his walk with the Irishwoman, who talked to him of many things, but when they reached the big house she disappeared.

Mr Grimes sent Tom to sweep the chimneys in a big house. There were so many and they were so crooked that soon Tom lost his way. At last, tired and hungry, he climbed down one of the chimneys and found he had come out in the wrong room. It was a pink and white bedroom and in the bed was a beautiful little girl.

While Tom looked at her she woke up, and seeing Tom all covered with soot, she screamed. Tom jumped out of the window and raced across the garden, while behind him everybody seemed to be chasing him.

In the end he reached the top of a steep cliff and he dragged himself to a cottage door and there inside was the kindest-looking old woman he had ever seen. She wore a red skirt, a shawl and a black scarf on her head. The old lady gave him hot milk and put him to bed.

As he slept, a magic thing happened to Tom. He tossed and turned and in his sleep heard the old Irishwoman call to him, 'Those that wish to be clean, clean they shall be.' Then, suddenly Tom was flinging off his clothes and swimming happily in the river. You see, the Irishwoman was really a fairy and had turned Tom from a chimney sweep into a tiny water baby.

Things to do and make

The children at Iken Hall rescued Sam from the chimney where he was stuck. Then they made a great mess of sooty footprints by the window to show Black Bob how he had escaped. It is fun to make footprints.

Footprints

You will need

powder paint

an old plate

a large sheet of plain paper

1 Mix the paint with water on the plate.

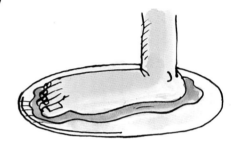

2 Stand your bare foot very carefully on the plate.

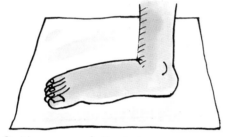

3 Now carefully take your foot and place it on the paper. You will see you have made a footprint.

4 Now fill your paper with footprints. Take care not to make a mess with the paint.

After you have made a pattern with your footprints, you could make a picture with your handprints. Why not make a picture of a swan?

A swan

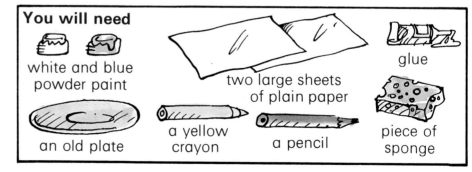

You will need

white and blue powder paint

an old plate

two large sheets of plain paper

a yellow crayon

a pencil

glue

piece of sponge

1 Mix the white paint with water in the plate.

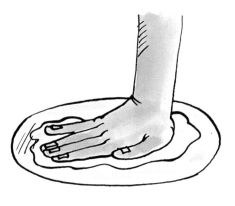

2 Put your hand in the paint,

3 Place your hand on the paper. Make six handprints and leave them to dry.

4 Draw a swan's head and body on the rest of the sheet of paper.

5 Paint the swan white.

6 Colour the beak and eye with yellow crayon.

7 Wash the plate. Mix the blue paint. Dip the sponge in the paint and paint the second piece of paper. This is your pond.

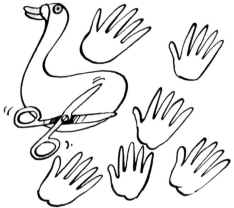

8 The handprints and the swan should now be dry. Cut them out carefully.

9 Glue the swan onto your pond. Now glue the handprints to make the tail. Copy the picture to help you. Now you have a swan on your pond.

35

A chimney sweep

Make a picture of a little sweep.

You will need

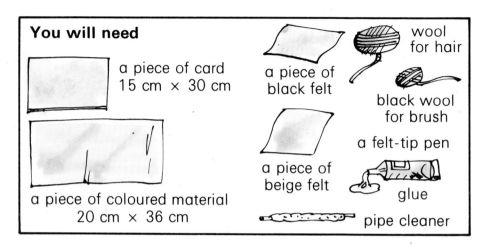

a piece of card
15 cm × 30 cm

a piece of coloured material
20 cm × 36 cm

a piece of
black felt

a piece of
beige felt

wool
for hair

black wool
for brush

a felt-tip pen

glue

pipe cleaner

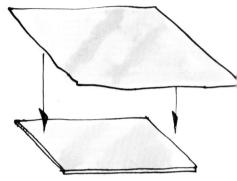

1 Lay the piece of coloured material on the piece of card.

2 Fold the material over the long sides first. Glue firmly.

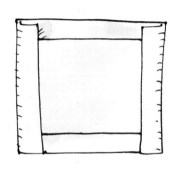

3 Now fold over the short sides and glue firmly.

4 From the beige felt cut out the following shapes: two arms, two hands, two legs and a head.

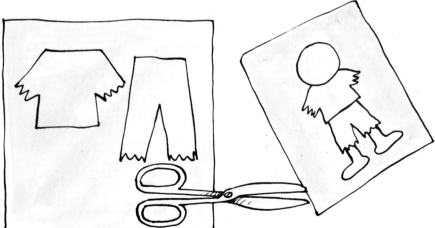

5 From the black felt cut out the little sweep's clothes: a ragged shirt and trousers.

6 Arrange all the shapes on your material card background to make a little sweep.

7 When you have arranged your picture, carefully glue it on the background.

8 Cut some lengths of wool for hair and glue on to your picture.

9 Use a felt-tip pen to colour in his eyes, nose and mouth.

10 Cut the black wool into 6 cm lengths and glue on to make a sweep's brush. Glue on a pipe cleaner for a handle.

Toffee apples

In *The Water Babies* there was one thing which Tom liked better than anything else. This was sweets. He loved the marvellous sea-lollipops, sea-apples, sea-oranges and sea-toffees.

We do not have a recipe for any of these 'sea' sweets, but you can make some toffee-apples which will be almost as good.

You will need

2 oz butter

1 lb brown sugar

½ ¼ pt water

apples

wooden sticks

1 tablespoon golden syrup

butter for greasing pan

1 Grease the saucepan with butter. Put all the ingredients, except the apples into the saucepan.

2 Heat gently until melted. Now boil rapidly for 5 minutes but stir to prevent it sticking.

3 Push the wooden sticks well into the apples.

4 Dip the apples into the toffee, swirl around until they are coated in toffee.

5 Leave to dry and harden on a baking tray.

The Sorcerer's Apprentice

Many years ago there lived an old sorcerer, a magic man, and his apprentice, a boy who was learning to be a sorcerer.

The Sorcerer gave the boy lessons in magic, but he also expected the house to be cleaned and errands to be run. There were no taps in the house, so each day the apprentice had to fill a large, round tank in his master's study. He had to walk to the river, fill up his two buckets with water and carry them carefully back to the house. Every time any water was used he had to go to the river and carry back heavy buckets of water.

Soon the apprentice began to get tired of cleaning the house, running errands and fetching water. He wanted to work magic himself. He listened outside the door but could only hear a few words from a spell. 'Oh dear,' he said, 'I will never be a sorcerer.'

One day the Sorcerer said 'I am going out for the day. When I come back I shall expect my tank to be full of water.' The boy was feeling tired and rather lazy. The tank was nearly empty and he knew it would take many journeys to the river with buckets to fill it up. Suddenly he saw a broom in the corner of the room, and he remembered his master had once used magic words to make the broom fetch water. What were these words? He thought for a moment or two, and then he remembered the words his master had used.

'Go, broom, go,' he commanded. 'Make the water flow.' As the boy spoke the magic spell, the broom sprang up, grew two arms, fetched a bucket and hopped to the river. Backwards and forwards hopped the broom from the river to the tank with the buckets of water.

The tank was filled in no time at all and the apprentice knew it was time to stop the magic. But he did not know the spell to end the broom's work. He looked everywhere, but he could not find the right spell.

'Swish, swash, stop the wash.' No, that was no use.

Ah, yes, now he remembered. 'Stop, broom, stop; Water's at the top.'

But still the broom kept hopping to the river with its bucket, and then filling the tank. By this time the tank was overflowing, and soon the room was flooded. The boy rushed out of the room to the shed and fetched an axe. Then he lifted the axe and struck the broom in two. But instead of stopping, there were now two brooms bringing in buckets of water. He struck again and again, and soon many brooms were hopping to and from the river.

The boy was frightened now and stood upon the table. 'Stop,' he called, 'Stop.'

The house was filled with water and all the furniture was floating. The apprentice was very, very frightened. Whatever was he going to say to his master?

Just then, the Sorcerer arrived home. He called in a loud voice, 'Cease, water, cease; Let there be peace.'

Instantly the water disappeared, the broom returned to its corner, and the furniture was back in its place. The other brooms vanished. Everything was peaceful.

The Sorcerer was very, very angry, but he knew that the apprentice had learnt his lesson. After that, the boy worked very hard and one day he became a famous sorcerer, too.

About the music

The Sorcerer's Apprentice was composed by Paul Dukas, a French composer, who was born in 1865 and died in 1935. The music was based on a poem by the German writer Goethe.

● Listen carefully to the music. Pretend that you are witches, wizards, goblins and fairies.

Group 1 You are the witches riding on your broomsticks. Remember to look after your black cats.

Group 2 You are the wizards putting snails and frogs' legs into your cauldron and casting spells. You turn people into frogs.

Group 3 You are the goblins. You peer out from behind the trees and then do an evil dance. You are very mischievous and annoy the wizard.

Group 4 You are dainty and beautiful fairies. You try to do good and dance round helping the wizards. You can pick flowers for your fairy queen.

Now change groups.

● When you are listening to *The Sorcerer's Apprentice* it is fun to draw the patterns of the music. Listen carefully and see if you can draw a pattern.

You will need
A large piece of paper
A pencil or a felt-tip pen
Everybody sit in a space round the room.
Do not look at anybody else.

The music will be played again. Listen carefully. Now draw the pattern of the music as you listen. When the music is loud make your pencil go *up*. When the music is quiet make your pencil go *down*. It is interesting to compare everybody's patterns. Do they go up and down in the same places?

About magic and magicians

The Sorcerer knew many, many spells. Here is a poem about magic spells.

Spells

I dance and dance without any feet –
This is the spell of the ripening wheat.

With never a tongue I've a tale to tell –
This is the meadow-grasses' spell.

I give you health without any fee –
This is the spell of the apple-tree.

I rhyme and riddle without any book –
This is the spell of the bubbling brook.

Without any legs I run for ever –
This is the spell of the mighty river.

I fall for ever and not at all –
This is the spell of the waterfall.

Without a voice I roar aloud –
This is the spell of the thunder-cloud.

No button or seam has my white coat –
This is the spell of the leaping goat.

I can cheat strangers with never a word –
This is the spell of the cuckoo-bird.

We have tongue in plenty but speak no names –
This is the spell of the fiery flames.

The creaking door has a spell to riddle –
I play a tune without any fiddle.

JAMES REEVES

Here is a poem about an alchemist. An alchemist is someone who can turn metals into gold; he is rather like a sorcerer.

The Alchemist

There lives an old man at the top of the street,
And the end of his beard reaches down to his feet,
And he's just the one person I'm longing to meet,
    I think that he sounds so exciting;
For he talks all the day to his tortoiseshell cat,
And he asks about this, and explains about that,
And at night he puts on a big wide-awake hat,
    And sits in the writing-room, writing.

He has worked all his life (and he's terribly old),
At a wonderful spell which says, 'Lo, and behold!
Your nursery fender is gold!' – and it's gold!
    (Or the tongs, or the rod for the curtain);
But somehow he hasn't got hold of it quite,
Or the liquid you pour on it first isn't right,
So that's why he works at it night after night,
    Till he knows he can do it for certain.

A. A. MILNE

The magic porridge pot

This is a story about a little girl who was given a magic porridge pot. When her Mummy used the magic words to start the pot cooking, she forgot the words to stop it.

Once there was a little girl who lived with her Mummy. She had no Daddy and the family were very poor. They had no money for new clothes and one day they found that there was nothing left to eat.

The little girl went into the woods to play but she was so hungry that she began to cry. Suddenly, an old woman in a long, grey cloak and hood came up to her.

'Why are you so unhappy?' she asked the little girl.

'Oh,' said the little girl, 'I am so unhappy because I haven't had any food for two days. I am so hungry.'

'Do not worry,' said the old woman. 'You shall not be hungry any more. I will give you this cooking pot. Whenever you are hungry just hold the pot and say, 'Cook, little pot, cook'. Then the little pot will cook as much porridge as you can eat. When you have finished just say, 'Stop, little pot, stop'.'

The little girl said, 'Thank you very much.' She was so hungry that she sat down on the grass at once and said, 'Cook, little pot, cook.'

Suddenly the pot started to bubble and to cook the most delicious porridge. When the pot was full, the little girl said 'Stop, little pot, stop.' The pot stopped cooking and the little girl went home and told her Mummy about the old lady and the porridge pot.

After that, whenever the little girl and her Mummy were hungry they just said 'Cook, little pot, cook' and the magic porridge pot gave them as much porridge as they could eat. It was delicious and they did enjoy it.

One day, the little girl was out for a walk when her Mummy felt hungry. Her Mummy said, 'Cook, little pot, cook.' At once the pot started to bubble and to cook the most delicious porridge. But soon she became very frightened because she had forgotten which

words she should use to tell the pot to stop cooking. The porridge began to spread over the cloth and down the table legs to the floor. The mother began to get very worried and tried all the magic words she knew, but not one was the right one.

Now the porridge was across the floor and out of the doorway. Soon all the houses in the street were full of porridge and it was running down the road. The people were very angry indeed and kept saying to the little girl's Mummy, 'Why don't you *do* something to stop the porridge?'

By now the porridge was covering all the streets in the town. 'Slurp, slurp,' it said as it bubbled out of doorways and through streets.

Just then the little girl came back from her walk through the woods.

'Oh my, oh my!' she said, 'Whatever has happened?'

At that moment she saw her Mummy making her way through the sea of porridge towards her.

'Please help quickly,' said her Mummy. 'I cannot remember the magic words to stop our porridge pot.' At once the little girl said, 'Stop, little pot, stop.' The pot stopped cooking and everybody was happy. But it took a long, long time to clean all the houses.

Here are two nursery rhymes about porridge.

Mary Ann, Mary Ann,
Make the porridge in a pan;
Make it thick, make it thin,
Make it any way you can.

Pease porridge hot, pease porridge cold,
Pease porridge in the pot, nine days old.
Some like it hot, some like it cold,
Some like it in the pot, nine days old.

Do you like porridge for breakfast? What do you put on your porridge? Some people like creamy milk and brown sugar, and some people like syrup.

Things to do and make

Magician's clothes

A sorcerer is a magic man rather like a wizard or a magician. Here are some clothes to make for you to wear when you work magic spells and tricks.

Cloak

You will need

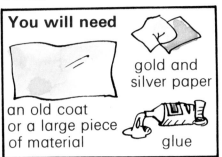

gold and silver paper

an old coat or a large piece of material

glue

1 Cut out some stars and moons in the gold and silver paper.

2 Glue the stars and moons on to your cloak.

Hat

You will need

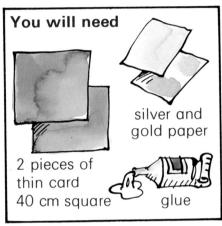

silver and gold paper

2 pieces of thin card 40 cm square

glue

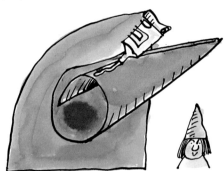

1 Draw a fan shape on one piece of card, cut it out and roll it into a cone to fit your head. Glue the edge.

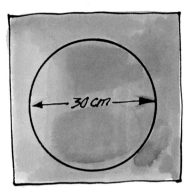

2 On the other piece of card draw a circle 30 cm wide.

30 cm

3 Draw another circle inside the first one, 23 cm wide (this may be changed to fit your head). Cut out the circles.

4 Snip around the inside edge, 10 mm, and bend up the tabs. Glue these up into the cone.

5 Cut out some stars and moons in gold and silver paper and glue these on to your hat.

Magic wand

You will need

black paint

a piece of thin white card
40 cm × 32 cm

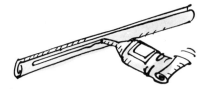

1 Roll the paper up carefully into a long tube and glue it.

2 Now paint your wand black. Leave about 6 cm white at each end.

Now you have a magic cloak, a hat and a wand.
You are all ready to be a sorcerer and make your spells.

Magic spells

Now you have made your sorcerer's outfit, you
will want to perform some magic tricks and spells.

1 The balloon trick

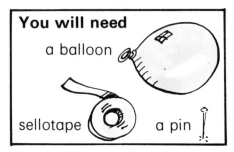

You will need

a balloon

sellotape   a pin

Blow the balloon up and tie the end. Stick a piece of sellotape on the blown-up balloon. Now stick a pin into the balloon through the sellotape. The balloon shouldn't burst if the sellotape is stuck firmly.

2 The egg cup trick

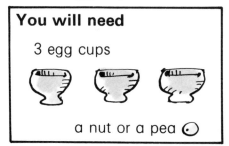

You will need

3 egg cups

a nut or a pea

Turn the three egg cups upside down.
Put the nut or pea under one of them.
Now say some magic words like 'Abracadabra' and move the egg cups around.
If you move them quickly enough your audience will forget which one is hiding the nut or pea.
But *you* must not forget.

3 The floating needle trick

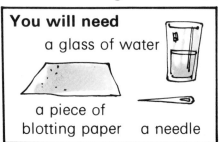

You will need

a glass of water

a piece of blotting paper   a needle

Put the piece of blotting paper carefully on the top of the water. Place the needle on to the blotting paper.
When the water has soaked through the blotting paper, the paper will sink to the bottom of the glass. The needle will stay floating on the surface.

Tricks with water

The little apprentice certainly made the water flow.
Here are some experiments to do with water. Make
sure *you* don't leave the tap running.

Trick 1

You will need

a basin of water

a cork

a pebble

a plastic clothes peg

a lump of dough

a twig

Put the cork in the water. Does it sink or float?
Put the pebble in the water. Does it sink or float?
Put the plastic clothes peg in the water. Does it sink or float?
Put the twig in the water. Does it sink or float?
Put the lump of dough in the water. Does it sink or float?

Trick 2

You will need

a piece of card

a plastic beaker

Fill the beaker with water.
Slide the piece of card over the top of the beaker.
Turn the beaker upside down. This should be done over a basin.
Now take your hand away.
What happens to the card and the water?

Trick 3

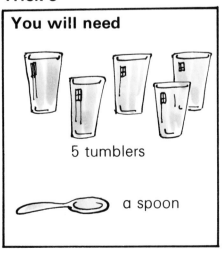

You will need

5 tumblers

a spoon

1 Fill one tumbler full of water.

2 Fill the next tumbler three-quarters full of water.

  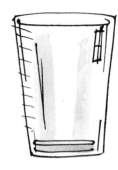

3 Fill the third tumbler half-full of water.

4 Fill the fourth tumbler one-quarter full of water.

5 Put just a very little water in the last tumbler.

6 Now tap the rims of the tumblers lightly with the spoon. Listen carefully to the different sounds they make. Can you make a tune?

Trick 4

You will need

5 milk bottles

Fill one bottle full of water.
Fill the next bottle three-quarters full of water.
Fill the third bottle half-full of water.

Fill the fourth bottle one-quarter full of water.
Put just a very little water in the last bottle.

Blow carefully over the bottles. Listen to the different sounds they make.
See if you can make up a tune.

48